Chapter books from Henry Holt and Company

◆

Three Little Robbers

CHRISTINE GRAHAM
illustrations by SUSAN BOASE

Henry Holt and Company ✦ New York

Henry Holt and Company, LLC
Publishers since 1866
175 Fifth Avenue
New York, New York 10010
www.HenryHoltKids.com

Library of Congress Cataloging-in-Publication Data
Graham, Christine.
Three little robbers / Christine Graham ; illustrations by Susan Boase.—1st ed.
p.   cm.
Summary: When Jo, Flo, and Mo try to rob the old lady who lives on the hill,
they find she has nothing at all, so they come up with a plan to help her
without stealing a single thing!
ISBN-13: 978-0-8050-8094-0 / ISBN-10: 0-8050-8094-5
[1. Robbers and outlaws—Fiction. 2. Behavior—Fiction.
3. Helpfulness—Fiction.] I. Boase, Susan, ill. II. Title.
PZ7.G751673Th 2007   [E]—dc22   2006033440

First Edition—2007 / Designed by Véronique Lefèvre Sweet
Printed in the United States of America on acid-free paper. ∞

1   3   5   7   9   10   8   6   4   2

Thanks to Lora, Brenda, Bobbie, and Jean

—C. G.

Dedicated to my junior high school art teacher,
Mr. Richard Cross, who taught me that making
marks is important work

—S. B.

Contents

◆

Three Little Robbers

✦ CHAPTER 1 ✦

The Robbers

Jo, Flo, and Mo were robbers who
lived on a lane.

Jo was strong.

Flo was loud.

Mo was quick.

They robbed people who came up the lane. They robbed people who came down the lane.

Soon no one came. The robbers had nothing.

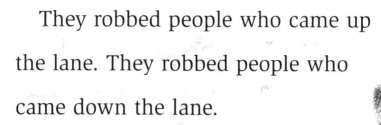

13

"I am hungry," said Jo.

"I am cold!" yelled Flo.

"I am bored," said Mo. "It is too dark to read."

"I know!" yelled Flo. "We can rob that old lady who lives on the hill. Jo can bang on the door. I can yell, 'Give us your things!' Mo can run away with the things."

✦ CHAPTER 2 ✦
The Old Lady

The robbers went up the hill to the old lady's little house. Jo banged on the door very hard.

The door crashed down.

The robbers stepped in. The house was dark and cold.

"What do you want?" asked a tiny voice.

"Give us food," said Jo.

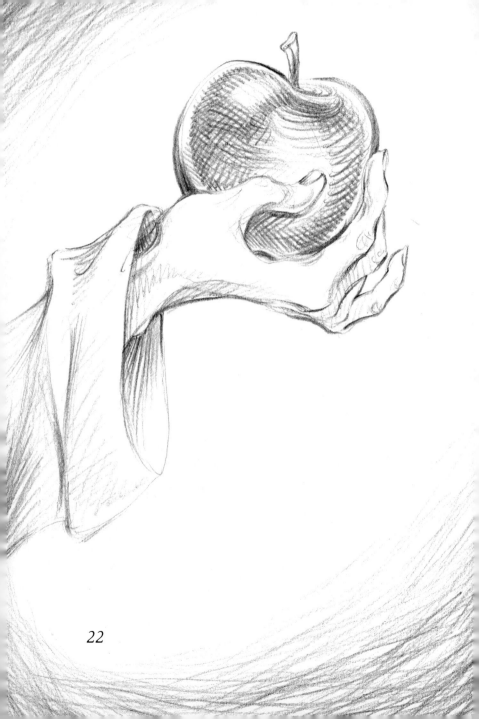

"I have one apple," said the tiny voice. "If you are hungry, you may have it."

"Oh," said Jo.

24

"Give us blankets!" yelled Flo.

"I have no blankets," said the tiny voice. "I have a cat. If you are cold, she will sit on your lap."

"Oh!" said Flo.

"Give us candles," said Mo.

"I have no candles," said the tiny

voice. "I open the curtains and let in

the moonlight."

27

"Oh," said Mo. "We will go away."

29

CHAPTER 3

The Long Night

The three robbers went out. Jo put
the door back. They walked up the
tallest hill and sat on a big rock.

"The old lady is hungry," said Jo.

"She is cold," said Flo.

"She needs light," said Mo.

"I know!" yelled Flo. "We will steal things for her."

"No," said Jo. "She would not like that."

"We are robbers," said Flo. "What else can we do?"

The cold, hungry robbers sat on the rock and thought all night.

✦ CHAPTER 4 ✦
The Milkmaid

The sun came up. The three robbers sat on the hill and watched the lane.

"Oh look," said Jo. "There is mud all over the lane. The milk wagon is stuck in the mud."

"Yes," said the milkmaid. "I pull and pull. The wagon stays stuck."

"I am strong. I can get it out," said Jo.

"Please do!" said the milkmaid.

Jo pushed and pulled. The wagon
did not move.

Jo pushed and pulled some more.
The wagon moved a little.

Jo rolled rocks under the wheels.

She pushed some more.

The milkmaid pushed, too. The wagon came out.

"Oh," said Jo. "That was fun."

"Thank you!" said the milkmaid.

She gave Jo a big, round cheese.

41

✦ CHAPTER 5 ✦

The Farmer

A farmer came up the lane with his sheep.

The sheep did not stay in the lane. They ran up the hills. They rolled down the hills. They played run-sheep-run across the lane.

"Oh!" yelled Flo. "The sheep are all over!"

"Yes," said the farmer. "I call and call. The sheep do not hear."

"I am loud!" yelled Flo.

"Call them!" said the farmer.

"Yo, sheep!" Flo yelled. The sheep came fast.

"That was fun!" yelled Flo.

"Thank you!" said the farmer. He gave Flo a soft wool blanket.

49

✦ CHAPTER 6 ✦
The Peddler

"Oh," said Mo. "There are candles rolling down the lane!"

"Oh no," said the peddler. "My candles are rolling away!"

The peddler ran after the candles.
He slipped on the candles and fell.

The peddler rubbed his knee. He
watched his candles roll down the
lane.

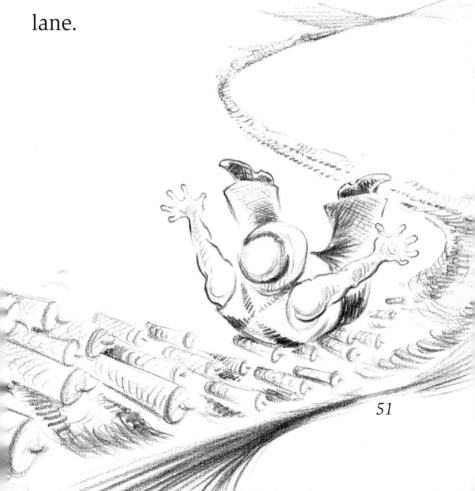

"I am quick," said Mo. "I will get your candles."

Mo ran. The candles rolled fast. Mo ran faster.

She jumped over the candles and stopped them.

She picked them up and took them to the peddler.

The peddler put them in his pack.

"That was fun," said Mo.

"Thank you!" said the peddler. He gave Mo some candles.

✦ CHAPTER 7 ✦

The Gifts

That night Jo took the cheese. Flo took the soft wool blanket. Mo took the candles. They went to the old lady's little house.

They knocked on the door. The door crashed down.

"Oh no," said the tiny voice. "I ate the apple. My cat is hunting. The moon is down. I have nothing."

"Oh yes," said Jo. "You have

cheese."

"You have a blanket!" yelled Flo.

"You have candles," said Mo.

Jo sliced the cheese. The cat smelled the cheese. She came up purring. She rubbed the robbers' legs and sat on their laps.

Flo wrapped the blanket around the old lady.

Mo handed her a bright candle.

"Oh my," said the old lady. "Oh,

thank you!"

She looked at the three robbers.
They were full. They were warm.
They were sleepy.

"I will tell you a story," said the
old lady. "Jo, Flo, and Mo were
robbers who lived on a lane. . . ."